HANUKAH MONEY

by Sholem Aleichem

translated and adapted by
Uri Shulevitz and Elizabeth Shub

illustrated by Uri Shulevitz

MULBERRY BOOKS • New York

Library of Congress Cataloging in Publication Data
Shulevitz, Uri (date), Hanukah money.
Summary: Two young brothers wonder how much money
they will receive from their relatives for Hanukkah.
[1. Jews—Fiction. 2. Hanukkah (Feast of Lights)—Fiction]
I. Shub, Elizabeth, joint author. II. Rabinowitz, Shalom, 1859-1916.
Hanuke gelt. III. Title. PZ7.S5594Han [E] 77-26693
ISBN 0-688-10993-4

To
Edward Friedman
Yehuda Mintz
Paul Perkal
Zeev and Sarah Shteininger
Henry and Ida Sulewic
Miriam Zucker and Family
and to the memory of
Israel Jomski
U. S.

Winter. Outdoors the frost burns. The snow-sealed windows are covered with delicate patterns. Indoors the heat warms the soul. The silver Hanukah lamp has been ready since morning. Father paces the room, chanting the

Evening Prayer. He goes to a drawer, takes out a candle, and still praying, turns to us, my younger brother Motl and me, and intones in Hebrew:

"Eee-oh! 'And the Lord stretched forth the heavens . . .' Eee-noo-oh!"

Father points toward the kitchen. We don't understand what he means.

"What? A match?" we ask.

"Mother! Call mother, to hear the blessings over the Hanukah candles."

We dash off, tripping over each other.

"Mother! Quick, the Hanukah lights!"

"A plague on me, Hanukah lights!" says mother and sets aside her work in the kitchen, where goose fat is frying and potato pancakes are sizzling. She hurries into the living room, followed by Breineh the cook, a dark woman with a moustache. Mother makes a pious face, and Breineh stands by the door, wiping her hands on her apron. She puts one hand up to her face and leaves a black smudge. Motl and I almost explode trying to keep from laughing.

Father carries a lighted candle to the Hanukah lamp, bows, and says the familiar blessing, which begins "Praised be Thou" and ends "to kindle the light of Hanukah!"

Mother answers piously, "Amen," and Breineh nods her head, making such a face that Motl and I don't dare look at each other.

"These candles we light to recall the miracles, the wonders, the battles, and the victories that Thou performedst for our forefathers in those days at this season . . ." father chants in his nasal tone, wandering back and forth across the room. He stops before the Hanukah lamp, and prays and prays and never stops praying. We can't wait until he finishes, because it is then that he will reach into his pocket for his wallet. We look at each other, poke each other.

"Motl, you ask for the Hanukah money."

"Why me?"

"Because you're younger."

"No, you should ask because you're older."

Father knows what we're talking about, but he pretends not to. Slowly he takes out his wallet and counts out money. Our hearts beat faster. We look at the ceiling, scratch behind our ears, pretend as if what is happening has nothing to do with us.

Father coughs. "Hmm. . . . Children, come here. Here is your Hanukah money."

We take it and walk away, slowly at first, like well-mannered boys, then faster and faster. We jump, we jig, and when we reach our room, do three somersaults, and end up hopping on one leg and singing:

"Eingeh, beingeh,

Stupeh, tseingeh,

Artseh, bartseh,

Goleh, shvartseh,

Eimeleh, reimeleh,

Beigeleh, feigeleh,

Hop!"

The door opens and Uncle Bennie walks in.

"Well, gang, it's time for Hanukah money!"

He puts his hand in his vest pocket, removes two coins and gives them to us.

Father takes a large sheet of paper and draws a checkerboard on it. He asks us to bring beans from the kitchen, black ones and white ones, to use as checkers. My brother Motl and I take out our dreidels and begin to play. Father and Uncle Bennie sit down to their game.

"One thing I will ask of you, Bennie," father says, "no tricks and no changes. That means: A move is a move!"

"A move is a move," Uncle Bennie repeats, and makes a move.

"A move is a move," father says, and jumps Uncle Bennie's piece.

"A move is a move," Uncle Bennie says, and jumps father's two pieces.

The deeper they get into the game, the more they chew their beards, shuffle their feet under the table, and softly hum the same tune.

"What's to be done, what's to be done, what's to be done?" intones father. "Shall I move here? He'll go there. If I move there, he'll go here."

"Move there, go here," choruses Uncle Bennie.

"Why should I be afraid?" father sings on. "If he takes this piece, I'll take two of his. But what if he is planning to take three pieces?"

"Three pieces, three pieces, three pieces," Uncle Bennie helps him along.

Mother comes from the kitchen, her face is red. She's followed by Breineh carrying a huge platter of steaming hot potato pancakes. Everyone goes to the table. My brother Motl and I, who were fighting a moment before, make up and settle down to the business of eating pancakes.

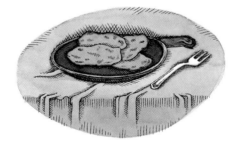

At night, I lie in bed and try to figure out how much money we would have if all the uncles and all the aunts and all the relatives gave us Hanukah money.

"Motl, are you asleep?"

"Yes. What is it?"

"How much Hanukah money, do you think, Uncle Moishe-Aaron will give us?"

"How should I know? Am I a prophet?"

A minute later: "Motl, are you asleep?"

"Yes. What now?"

"Does everyone have as many uncles and aunts as we do?"

"Maybe yes, maybe no."

Two minutes later: "Motl, are you asleep?"

"Y-e-s-s?"

"If you're asleep, how come you're talking to me?"

"You ask me a question, so I have to answer."

Three minutes later: "Motl, are you asleep?"

Tsss—Trrr—Khilkhilkhil—Tsss . . . Motl is snoring, snorting, whistling through his nose.

"Good morning, Aunt Pessl, good morning, Uncle Moishe-Aaron!" we burst out together.

Aunt Pessl, a tiny woman with one black eyebrow and one white, helps us take off our coats, unwinds our scarves, and makes us blow our noses into her apron.

"Blow!" she says. "Good, good, blow real good! Don't be stingy! More! More! That's it!"

Uncle Moishe-Aaron, in a tattered bathrobe with a quilted cotton skullcap on his head, cotton in one ear, and a sparse moustache, rubs his hands. Aunt Pessl sits down facing us, her hands on her heart, and starts her usual catechism.

"What's father doing?"

"Nothing."

"What's mother doing?"

"Nothing."

"Rendered fat?"

"Rendered."

"Fried pancakes?"

"Fried."

"Uncle Bennie came?"

"Came."

"Played checkers?"

"Played."

And so on.

Aunt Pessl blows our noses again and calls out to Uncle Moishe-Aaron, "Moishe-Aaron, Hanukah money for the children!"

Uncle Moishe-Aaron doesn't hear; he rubs his hands and continues croaking out the Morning Prayer:

"Blessed art Thou, O Lord, who healest all flesh, and workest wonders."

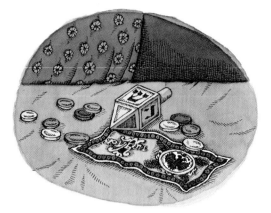

Aunt Pessl doesn't give up. She reminds him again, "Moishe-Aaron, Hanukah money for the children!"

"Hah?" says Uncle Moishe-Aaron, taking out the cotton from one ear and putting it into the other.

"Hanukah money for the children!" Aunt Pessl shouts right into his ear.

"Oh, my stomach! My stomach!" moans Uncle Moishe-Aaron and he holds his stomach with both hands. "Hanukah money? What do children want with money? What will you do with the money? Hah? Spend it, waste it, hah? How much did your father give you, hah?"

"Me a ruble," I say, "and him a half."

"A ruble? Hmm. . . . Children are being spoiled, ruined! What will you do with a ruble? Get change? Spend it? Hah? Don't change it! Do you hear what I say? Don't change it! Are you going to change it, hah?"

"Yes change it, no change it—is it any of your business?" Aunt Pessl intervenes. "Give them what's coming to them and let them go in good health."

Uncle Moishe-Aaron opens all the drawers of a dresser, and finally digs out some old coins, all the while talking to himself, "Nowadays children are being spoiled, ruined, totally ruined!"

He gives us the coins. Aunt Pessl blows our noses one last time, bundles us into our coats, and we're on our way.

"Well, Motl, let's get to work, let's figure out how much Hanukah money we've got. First you be quiet and I'll count mine, then you'll count yours."

I begin to count. "One ruble, and three chetvertaks, and four grivenniks, and five piataks, and six kopeks—how much is that all together? A ruble, and three chetvertaks, and four grivenniks, and five piataks, and six kopeks. . . ."

Motl is impatient. He doesn't want to wait until I've finished. He transfers the coins from one hand to the other,

counting. "One chetvertak and one chetvertak makes two chetvertaks, and another chetvertak makes three chetvertaks, and two grivenniks is three chetvertaks and two grivenniks, and a piatak and another piatak and another piatak makes two piataks and three grivenniks. I mean, three piataks and two chetvertaks. Oh, I'll have to start from the beginning!"

And he starts all over again.

We count and we count and we can't add up our money. We figure and we figure and we can't figure it out. . . .

Breineh comes in from the kitchen carrying a huge platter of rubles. She isn't walking, she's floating and singing, "These candles we light to recall the miracles. . . ."

Motl swallows rubles like pancakes.

"Motl," I cry out, "Motl, what are you doing? Eating rubles?"

I awake, sit up . . . a dream. Tfoo-tfoo-tfoo, I spit three times.

And go back to sleep.

GLOSSARY

chetvertak (*chet* ver tak) = 25 kopeks

grivennik (*griv* nik) = 10 kopeks

kopek (*ko* pek) = 1/100 of a ruble

piatak (*pya* tak) = 5 kopeks

ruble (*roo* b'l) = 100 kopeks

"Eingeh, beingeh . . ." (page 13)
is a popular Yiddish nonsense verse.